GREATEST POWER OF YOUR MIND

GREATEST POWER OF YOUR MIND

Joseph Murphy

PRABHAT PRAKASHAN

Published by
PRABHAT PRAKASHAN PVT. LTD.
4/19 Asaf Ali Road,
New Delhi-110 002 (INDIA)
e-mail: prabhatbooks@gmail.com

ISBN 978-93-5266-832-8
GREATEST POWER OF YOUR MIND
by Joseph Murphy

Edition
2024

Paperback Price
₹ 300.00 (Rupees Three Hundred only)

Printed at
R-Tech Offset Printers, Delhi

Contents

1

The Power of the Subconscious

Everyone is definitely concerned with the healing of bodily conditions and human affairs. What is it that heals? Where is this healing power? These are questions asked by everyone. The answer is that this healing power is in the subconscious mind of each person, and a changed mental attitude on the part of the sick person releases this healing power.

No mental or religious science practitioner, psychologist, psychiatrist, or medical doctor ever healed a patient. There is an old saying, "The doctor dresses the wound, but God heals it." The psychologist or psychiatrist proceeds to remove the mental blocks in the patient so that the healing principle may be released, restoring the patient to health. Likewise, the surgeon removes the physical block enabling the healing currents to function normally. No physician, surgeon, or mental science practitioner claims, "he healed the patient." The one healing power is called by many names—Nature, Life, God, Creative Intelligence, and Subconscious Power.

No mental or religious science practitioner, psychologist, psychiatrist, or medical doctor ever healed a patient. There is an old saying, "The doctor dresses the wound, but God heals it."

There are many different methods used to remove the mental, emotional, and physical blocks which inhibit the flow of the healing life Everyone is definitely concerned with the healing of bodily conditions and human affairs. What is it that heals? Where is this healing power? These are questions asked by everyone. The answer is that this healing power is in the subconscious mind of each person, and a changed mental attitude on the part of the sick person releases this healing power.

There are many different methods used to remove the mental, emotional, and physical blocks which inhibit the flow of the healing life Everyone is definitely concerned with the healing of bodily conditions and human affairs.

No mental or religious science practitioner, psychologist, psychiatrist, or medical doctor ever healed a patient. There is an old saying, "The doctor dresses the wound, but God heals it." The psychologist or psychiatrist proceeds to remove the mental blocks in the patient so that the healing principle may be released, restoring the patient to health. Likewise, the surgeon removes the physical block enabling the healing currents to function normally. No physician, surgeon, or mental science practitioner claims, "he healed the patient." The one healing power is called by many names—Nature, Life, God, Creative Intelligence, and Subconscious Power.

Likewise, the surgeon removes the physical block enabling the healing currents to function normally. No physician, surgeon, or mental science practitioner claims, "he healed the patient."

There are many different methods used to remove the mental, emotional, and physical blocks which inhibit the flow of the healing life principle animating all of us. The healing principle resident in your subconscious mind can and will, if properly directed by you or some other person, heal your mind and body of all disease. This healing principle is operative in all men regardless of caste creed, colour, or race. You do not have to belong to some particular church in order to use and participate in this healing process. Your subconscious will heal the burn or cut on your hand even though you profess to be an atheist or agnostic.

> ***There are many different methods used to remove the mental, emotional, and physical blocks which inhibit the flow of the healing life principle animating all of us.***

The modern mental therapeutic

procedure is based on the truth that the infinite intelligence and power of your subconscious mind responds according to your faith. Mental science practitioners or ministers follows the injunction of the Religions books. They go into a private place, their minds, relax, let go, and think of the infinite healing presence within them. They close their minds to all outside distractions as well as appearances, and then quietly and knowingly turns over a request or desire to the subconscious mind, realizing that the intelligence of the mind will provide answers according to specific needs.

Mental science practitioners or ministers follows the injunction of the Religions books. They go into a private place, their minds, relax, let go, and think of the infinite healing presence within them.

The most wonderful thing to know is this: Imagine the end desired and feel its reality;

then the infinite life principle will respond to your conscious choice and your conscious request. This is the meaning, *"believe you have received, and you shall receive".* This is what the modern mental scientist does when practicing prayer therapy.

Single Healing Process

There is only one universal healing principle operating through everything—the cat, the dog, the tree, the grass, the wind, the earth—for everything is alive. This life principle operates through the animal, vegetable, and mineral kingdoms as instinct and the law of growth. The human mind is consciously aware of

> ***There is only one universal healing principle operating through everything—the cat, the dog, the tree, the grass, the wind, the earth—for everything is alive.***

this life principle, and can consciously direct it to bless itself in countless ways.

There are many different approaches, techniques, and methods in using the universal power, but there is only one process of healing, which is faith, for *according to your faith* is it done unto you.

> ***There are many different approaches, techniques, and methods in using the universal power, but there is only one process of healing, which is faith, for according to your faith is it done unto you***

The Belief Law

The law of life is belief. All religions of the world represent forms of belief, and these beliefs are explained in many ways. What do you believe about yourself, life, and the universe? It is done unto you as you believe.

Belief is a thought in your mind, which

causes the power of your subconscious to be distributed into all phases of your life according to your thinking habits. You must realize that the religious books are not talking about your belief in some ritual, ceremonial, form, institution, or formula. It is talking about *belief* itself. The belief of your mind is simply the thought of your mind. *If thou canst believe, all things are possible to him that believeth.*

(MARK 9:23).

It is foolish to believe in something that will hurt or harm you. Remember, it is not the thing believed in that hurts or harms you, but the belief or thought in your mind that creates the result.

It is foolish to believe in something that will hurt or harm you. Remember, it is not the thing believed in that hurts or harms you, but the belief or thought in your mind that creates the result. All your experiences, all your actions, and all the events and circumstances of your life are but the reflections and reactions to your own thought.

Prayer therapy: A scientifically directed combined function of the conscious and subconscious mind

Prayer therapy is the synchronized, harmonious, and intelligent function of the conscious and subconscious levels of mind specifically directed for a definite purpose. In scientific prayer or prayer therapy, you must know what you are doing and why you are doing it. You trust the law of healing. Prayer therapy is sometimes referred to as mental treatment,or scientific prayer.

> ***Prayer therapy is the synchronized, harmonious, and intelligent function of the conscious and subconscious levels of mind specifically directed for a definite purpose.***

In prayer therapy you consciously choose a certain idea, mental picture, or plan which you desire to experience. You realize your capacity to convey this idea or mental image to your subconscious by feeling the reality of the state assumed. As you remain faithful in your mental attitude, your prayer will be answered. Prayer therapy is a definite mental action for a definite specific purpose.

You realize your capacity to convey this idea or mental image to your subconscious by feeling the reality of the state assumed.

Let's suppose that you decide to heal a certain difficulty by prayer therapy. You are aware that your problem or sickness, whatever it may be, must be caused by negative thoughts charged with fear and lodged in your subconscious mind, and that if you can succeed in cleansing your mind of these thoughts, you will get a healing.

You, therefore, turn to the healing power

within your own subconscious mind and remind yourself of its infinite power and intelligence and its capacity to heal all conditions. As you dwell on these truths, your fear will begin to dissolve, and the recollection of these truths also corrects the erroneous beliefs.

> ***You give thanks for the healing that you know will come, and then you keep your mind off the difficulty until you feel guided, after an interval, to pray again.***

You give thanks for the healing that you know will come, and then you keep your mind off the difficulty until you feel guided, after an interval, to pray again. While you are praying, it is essential that you refuse to give any power to any negative conditions or to admit for a second that the healing will not come. This attitude of mind brings about the harmonious union of the conscious and subconscious mind, which releases the healing power.

Faith Healing, Meaning and Its Work

What is popularly termed faith healing is not the faith mentioned in the religious books, which means a knowledge of the inter-action of the conscious and subconscious mind. Faith healers are people who heal without any real scientific understanding of the powers and forces involved. They may claim that they have a special gift of healing, and the sick person's blind belief in these powers may bring results.

> ***What is popularly termed faith healing is not the faith mentioned in the religious books, which means a knowledge of the inter-action of the conscious and subconscious mind.***

Voodoo doctors in primitive societies may heal by incantations, or a person may be healed by touching the so-called bones of saints, or anything else, which cause the patients to honestly believe in the method or process.

Any method which causes one to move from fear and worry to faith and expectancy will heal. There are many persons, who my claim that because a personal theory produces results, it is, therefore, the correct one. This, as already explained in this chapter, cannot be true.

To illustrate how blind faith works: Let's look at the Swiss physician, Franz Anton Mesmer. In 1776 he claimed many cures when he stroked diseased bodies with artificial magnets.

To illustrate how blind faith works: Let's look at the Swiss physician, Franz Anton Mesmer. In 1776 he claimed many cures when he stroked diseased bodies with artificial magnets. Later on he threw away his magnets and evolved the theory of animal magnetism. This he held to be a fluid which pervades the universe, but is most active in the human organism.

He claimed that this magnetic fluid,

which was going forth from him to his patients healed them. People flocked to him, and many miraculous cures were affected.

Mesmer moved to Paris, and while there the Government appointed a commission composed of physicians and members of the Academy of Science, of which Benjamin Franklin was a member, to investigate his cures. The report admitted the leading facts claimed by Mesmer, but held that there was no evidence to prove the correctness of his magnetic fluid theory, and said the effects were due to the imagination of the patients.

Mesmer moved to Paris, and while there the Government appointed a commission composed of physicians and members of the Academy of Science, of which Benjamin Franklin was a member, to investigate his cures.

Soon after this,

Mesmer was driven into exile, and died in 1815. Shortly afterwards, Dr. Braid of Manchester undertook to show that magnetic fluid had nothing to do with the production of the healings of Dr. Mesmer. Dr. Braid discovered that patients could be thrown into hypnotic sleep by suggestion, during which many of the well-known phenomena ascribed to magnetism by Mesmer could be produced.

You can readily see that all these cures were undoubtedly brought about by the active imagination of the patients together with a powerful suggestion of health to their subconscious minds.

You can readily see that all these cures were undoubtedly brought about by the active imagination of the patients together with a powerful suggestion of health to their subconscious minds. All this could be termed blind faith as there was no understanding in those days as to how the cures were brought about.

Subjective Faith and its Meaning

You will recall the proposition, which need not be repeated at length, that the subjective or subconscious mind of an individual is as amenable to the control of his own conscious or objective mind as it is by the suggestions of another. It follows that whatever may be your objective belief, if you will assume to have faith actively or passively, your subconscious mind will be controlled by the suggestion, and your desire will be fulfilled. The faith

You will recall the proposition, which need not be repeated at length, that the subjective or subconscious mind of an individual is as amenable to the control of his own conscious or objective mind as it is by the suggestions of another.

required in mental healings is purely subjective.

In the healing of the body it is, of course, desirable to secure the concurrent faith of both the conscious and subconscious mind. However, it is not always essential if you will enter into a state of passivity and receptivity by relaxing the mind and the body and getting into a sleepy state. In this drowsy state your passivity becomes receptive to subjective impression.

In the healing of the body it is, of course, desirable to secure the concurrent faith of both the conscious and subconscious mind.

Recently, I was asked, "How is it that I got a healing through a priest? I did not believe what he said when he told me that there is no such thing as disease and that matter does not exist."

This man at first thought his intelligence was being insulted, and he protested against such a palpable absurdity. The explanation is simple. He was quieted by soothing words and told to get into a perfectly passive condition, to say nothing, and think of nothing for the time being. His minister also became passive, and affirmed quietly, peacefully, and constantly for about one half hour that this man would have perfect health, peace, harmony, and wholeness. He felt immense relief and was restored to health.

> ***He was quieted by soothing words and told to get into a perfectly passive condition, to say nothing, and think of nothing for the time being.***

It is easy to see that his subjective faith had been manifested by his passivity under treatment, and the suggestions of perfect healthfulness by the minister were conveyed to his subconscious mind. The two subjective minds were then en rapport. The minister was not handicapped by antagonistic autosuggestions of the patient arising from objective doubt of the power of the healer or the correctness of the theory. In this sleepy, drowsy state the conscious mind resistance is reduced to a minimum, and results followed. The subconscious mind of the patient being necessarily controlled by such suggestion exercised its functions in accordance therewith, and a healing followed.

Absent Treatment-what it Means

> ***Suppose you law learned that your mother was sick in New York City and you lived in Los Angeles.***

Suppose you law learned that your mother was sick in New York City and you lived in Los Angeles. Your mother would not be physically present where you are, but you could pray for her. *(It is the Father within which doeth the work.* (JOHN 14:10)

The creative law of mind (subconscious

mind) serves you and will do the work. Its response to you is automatic. Your treatment is for the purpose of inducing an inner realization of health and harmony in your mentality. This inner realization, acting through the subconscious mind, operates through your mother's subconscious mind as there is but one creative mind. Your thoughts of health, vitality, and perfection operate through the one universal subjective mind, and set a law in motion on the subjective side of life that manifests through her body as a healing.

In the mind principle there is no time or space. It is the same mind that operates through your mother no matter where she may be.

In the mind principle there is no time or space. It is the same mind that operates through your mother no matter where she may be. In reality there is no absent treatment as opposed to present treatment for the universal mind is omnipresent. You do not try to send out thoughts or hold a thought. Your treatment is a conscious movement of thought, and as you become conscious of the qualities of health, well-being, and relaxation, these qualities will be resurrected in the experience of your mother, and results will follow.

The healing presence is right where my mother is. Her bodily condition is but a reflection of her thought-life like shadows cast on the screen.

The following is a perfect example of what is called absent treatment. For example, a listener of our radio program in Los Angeles prayed as follows for her mother in New York who had a coronary thrombosis: "The healing presence is right where my mother is. Her bodily condition is but a reflection of her thought-life like shadows cast on the screen. I know that in order to change the images on the screen I must change the projection reel. My mind is the projection reel, and I now project in my own mind the image of wholeness, harmony, and perfect health for my mother. The infinite healing presence which created my mother's body and all her organs is now saturating every atom of her being, and a river of peace flows through every cell of her body. The doctors are divinely guided and directed, and whoever touches my mother is guided to do the right thing. I know that disease has no ultimate reality; if it had, no one could be healed. I now align myself with the infinite principle of love and life, and I know and decree that harmony, health, and peace are now being expressed in my mother's body."

> ***The infinite healing presence which created my mother's body and all her organs is now saturating every atom of her being, and a river of peace flows through every cell of her body.***

She prayed in the above manner several times daily, and her mother had a most remarkable recovery after a few days, much to the amazement of her specialist. He complimented her on her great faith in the power of God.

The conclusion arrived at in the daughter's mind set; the creative law of mind in motion on the subjective side of life, which manifested itself through her mother's body as perfect health and harmony.

The conclusion arrived at in the daughter's mind set; the creative law of mind in motion on the subjective side of life, which manifested itself through her mother's body as perfect health and harmony. What the daughter felt as true about her mother was simultaneously resurrected in the experience of her mother.

Kinetic Action of the Subconscious Mind and its Release

A psychologist friend of mine told me that one of his lungs was infected. X rays and analysis showed the presence of tuberculosis. At night before going to sleep he would quietly affirm, "Every cell, nerve, tissue, and muscle of my lungs are now being made whole, pure, and perfect. My whole body is being restored to health and harmony."

> ***A psychologist friend of mine told me that one of his lungs was infected. X rays and analysis showed the presence of tuberculosis.***

These are not his exact words, but they represent the essence of what he affirmed. A complete healing followed in about a month's time. Subsequent X rays showed a perfect healing.

I wanted to know his method, so I asked

him why he repeated the words prior to sleep. Here is his reply, "The kinetic action of the subconscious mind continues throughout your sleep-time period. Hence, give the subconscious mind something good to work on as you drop off into slumber." This was a very wise answer. In thinking of harmony and perfect health, he never mentioned his trouble by name.

I strongly suggest that you cease talking about your ailments or giving them a name. The only sap from which they draw life is your attention and fear of them.

I strongly suggest that you cease talking about your ailments or giving them a name. The only sap from which they draw life is your attention and fear of them. Like the above mentioned psychologist, become a mental surgeon. Then your troubles will be cut off like dead branches are pruned from a tree. If you are constantly naming your aches and symptoms, you inhibit the kinetic action, which means the release of the healing power and energy of your subconscious mind. Furthermore, by the law of your own mind, these imaginings tend to take shape, *As the thing I greatly feared.* Fill your mind with the great truths of life and walk forward in the light of love.

Aids to Good Health : A Gist

1. Find out what it is that heals you. Realize that correct directions given to your subconscious mind will heal your mind and body.

2. Develop a definite plan for turning over your requests or desires to your subconscious mind.

3. Imagine the end desired and feel its reality. Follow it through, and you will get definite results.

4. Decide what belief is. Know that belief is a thought in your mind, and what you think you create.

5. It is foolish to believe in sickness and something to hurt or to harm you. Believe in perfect health, prosperity, peace, wealth, and divine guidance.

6. Great and noble thoughts upon which you habitually dwell become great acts.

7. Apply the power of prayer therapy in your life. Choose a certain plan, idea, or mental picture. Mentally and emotionally unite with that idea, and as you remain faithful to your mental attitude, your prayer will be answered.

8. Always remember, if you really want the power to heal, you can have it through faith, which means a knowledge of the working of your conscious and subconscious mind. Faith comes with understanding.

9. Blind faith means that a person may get results in healing without any scientific

understanding of the powers and forces involved.

10. Learn to pray for your loved ones who may be ill. Quiet your mind, and your thoughts of health, vitality, and perfection operating through the one universal subjective mind will be felt and resurrected in the mind of your loved one.

2

Remaining Young & Energetic You Ever

Your subconscious mind never grows old. It is timeless, ageless, and endless. It is a part of the universal mind of God, which was never born, and it will never die.

Fatigue or old age cannot be predicated on any spiritual quality or power. Patience, kindness, veracity, humility, good will, peace, harmony, and brotherly love are attributes and qualities that never grow old. If you continue to generate these qualities here on this plane of life, you will always remain young in spirit.

I remember reading an article in one of our magazines some years ago, which stated that a group of eminent medical men at the De Courcy Clinic, in Cincinnati, Ohio, reported that years alone are not responsible for bringing about degenerative disorders. These same physicians stated that it is the fear of time, not time itself, that has a harmful aging effect on our minds and

I remember reading an article in one of our magazines some years ago, which stated that a group of eminent medical men at the De Courcy Clinic, in Cincinnati, Ohio, reported that years alone are not responsible for bringing about degenerative disorders.

bodies, and that the neurotic fear of the effects of time may well be the cause of premature aging.

During the many years of my public life, I have had occasion to study the biographies of the famous men and women who have continued their productive activities into the years well beyond the normal span of life. Some of them achieve their greatness in old age. At the same time, it has been my privilege to meet and to know countless individuals of no prominence who, in their lesser sphere, belonged to those hardy mortals who have proved that old age of itself does not destroy the creative powers of the mind and body.

During the many years of my public life, I have had occasion to study the biographies of the famous men and women who have continued their productive activities into the years well beyond the normal span of life.

He Had Grown Old in his Thought Life

A few years ago I called on an old friend in London, England. He was over 80 years of age, very ill, and obviously was yielding to his advancing years. Our conversation revealed his physical weakness, his sense of frustration, and a general deterioration almost approaching lifelessness. His cry was that he was useless and that no one wanted him. With an expression of hopelessness he betrayed his false philosophy, "We are born, grow up, become old, good for nothing, and that's the end."

A few years ago I called on an old friend in London, England. He was over 80 years of age, very ill, and obviously was yielding to his advancing years.

This mental attitude of futility and worthlessness was the chief reason for his sickness. He was looking forward only to senescence, and after that—nothing. Indeed, he had grown old in his thought life, and his subconscious mind brought about all the evidence of his habitual thinking.

With Age Comes Wisdom

Unfortunately, many people have the same attitude as this unhappy man. They are afraid of what they term "old age," the end, and extinction, which really means that they are afraid of life. Yet, life is endless. Age is not the flight of years, but the dawn of wisdom.

> ***Unfortunately, many people have the same attitude as this unhappy man. They are afraid of what they term "old age," the end, and extinction, which really means that they are afraid of life. Yet, life is endless.***

Wisdom is an awareness of the tremendous spiritual powers in your subconscious mind and the knowledge of how to apply these powers to lead a full and happy life. Get it out of your head once and for all that 65, 75, or 85 years of age is synonymous with the end for you or anybody else.

It can be the begin¬ning of a glorious, fruitful, active, and most productive life pattern, better than you have ever experienced. Believe this, expect it, and your subconscious will bring it to pass.

It can be the begin¬ning of a glorious, fruitful, active, and most productive life pattern, better than you have ever experienced.

Accept Change

Old age is not a tragic occurrence. What we call the aging process is really change. It is to be welcomed joyfully and gladly as each phase of human life is a step forward on the path that has no end. We have powers that transcend our bodily powers. We have senses that transcend the five physical senses.

Scientists today are finding positive indisputable evidence that something conscious in us can leave our present body and travel thousands of miles to see, hear, touch, and speak to people even though our physical body never leaves the couch on which it reclines.

> ***Our life is spiritual and eternal. We need never grow old for Life, or God, cannot grow old. The Bible says that God is Life.***

Our life is spiritual and eternal. We need never grow old for Life, or God, cannot grow old. The Bible says that God is Life. Life is self-renewing, eternal, indestructible, and is the reality of all humans.

Survival Itself is the Proof

The evidence gathered by the psychical research societies both in Great Britain and America is overwhelming. You may go into any large metropolitan library and get volumes on The Proceedings of the Psychical Research Society based on findings of distinguished scientists on survival following so-called death. You will find a startling report on scientific experiments establishing the reality of life after death in The Case for Psychic Survival by Hereward Carrington, Director of the American Psychical Institute.

> ***You will find a startling report on scientific experiments establishing the reality of life after death in The Case for Psychic Survival by Hereward Carrington, Director of the American Psychical Institute.***

Life is

A woman asked Thomas Edison, the

electrical wizard, "Mr. Edison, what is electricity?"

He replied, "Madame, electricity is. Use it."

> ***Scientists cannot see an electron with their eyes, yet they accept it as a scientific fact, because it is the only valid con¬clusion which coincides with other experimental evidence.***

Electricity is a name we give an invisible power that we do not fully comprehend, but we learn all we can about the principle of electricity and its uses. We use it in countless ways.

Scientists cannot see an electron with their eyes, yet they accept it as a scientific fact, because it is the only valid con¬clusion which coincides with other experimental evidence. We cannot see life. However, we know we are alive. Life is, and we are here to express it in all its beauty and glory.

Mind and Spirit are Always Young

Religious books syas, *And this is life eternal, that they might know thee the only true God.*

If you think or believe that the earthly cycle of birth, adolescence, youth, maturity, and old age is all there is to life, you are mistaken. For you, there is no anchor, no hope, no vision, and life has no meaning.

If you think or believe that the earthly cycle of birth, adolescence, youth, maturity, and old age is all there is to life, you are mistaken. For you, there is no anchor, no hope, no vision, and life has no meaning.

This type of belief brings frustration, stagnation, cynicism, and a sense of hopelessness resulting in neurosis and mental aberrations of all kinds. If you cannot play a fast game of tennis, or swim as fast as your son, or if your body has slowed down, or you walk with a slow step, remember life is always clothing itself anew. What we call death is but a journey to a new city in another dimension of Life.

> ***I say to men and women in my lectures that they should accept what we call old age gracefully. Age has its own glory, beauty, and wisdom that belong to it.***

I say to men and women in my lectures that they should accept what we call old age gracefully. Age has its own glory, beauty, and wisdom that belong to it. Peace, love, joy, beauty, happiness, wisdom, good will, and understanding are qualities that never grow old or die.

Ralph Waldo Emerson, poet and philosopher, said, "We do not count a man's years until he has nothing else to count."

Your character, the quality of your mind, your faith, and your convictions are not subject to decay.

Being Young is a State of Mind

I give public lectures in Caxton Hall, London, England, every few years, and following one of these lectures, a surgeon said to me, "I am 84 years of age. I operate every morning, visit patients in the afternoons, and I write for medical and other scientific journals in the evening."

> ***His attitude was that he was as useful as he believed himself to be, and that he was as young as his thoughts.***

His attitude was that he was as useful as he believed himself to be, and that he was as young as his thoughts. He said to me, "It's true what you said, `We are as strong as we thinks we are, and as valuable as we think he are.'"

This surgeon has not surrendered to advancing years. He knows that he is immortal. His final comment to me was, "If I should pass on tomorrow, I would be operating on people in the next dimension, not with a surgeon's scalpel, but with mental and spiritual surgery."

Your Gray Hairs are Signs of Wisdom

> ***Don't ever quit a job and say, "I am retired; I am old; I am finished." That would be stagnation, death, and you would be finished. Some people are old at 30, while others are young at 80.***

Don't ever quit a job and say, "I am retired; I am old; I am finished." That would be stagnation, death, and you would be finished. Some people are old at 30, while others are young at 80. The mind is the master weaver, the architect, the designer, and the sculptor. George Bernard Shaw was active at 90, and the artistic quality of his mind had not relaxed from active duty.

I meet men and women who tell me that some employers almost slam the door in their faces when they say they are over 40. This attitude on the part of the employers is to be considered cold, callous, evil, and completely void of compassion and understanding. The total emphasis seems to be on youth, i.e., you must be under 35 years of age to receive con¬sideration. The reasoning behind this is certainly very shallow. If the employer would stop and think, he would realize that the man or woman was not selling his age or gray hair, rather, he was willing to give of his talents, his experience, and his wisdom gathered through years of experience in the market place of life.

> ***The total emphasis seems to be on youth, i.e., you must be under 35 years of age to receive con¬sideration. The reasoning behind this is certainly very shallow.***

Age is a Property

Your age should be a distinct asset to any organization, because of your practice and application through the years of the principles of the Golden Rule and the law of love and good will. Your gray hair, if you have any, should stand for greater wisdom, skill, and understanding. Your emotional and spiritual maturity should be a tremendous blessing to any organization.

People should not be asked to resign at 65 years of age. That is the time of life when they could be most useful in handling personnel problems, making plans for the future, making decisions...

People should not be asked to resign at 65 years of age. That is the time of life when they could be most useful in handling personnel problems, making plans for the future, making decisions, and guiding others in the realm of creative ideas based on their experience and insight into the nature of the business.

Be Your Age

A motion-picture writer in Hollywood told me that he had to write scripts that would cater to the twelve-year-old mind. This is a tragic state of affairs if the great masses of people are expected to become emotionally and spiritually mature. It means that the emphasis is placed on youth in spite of the fact that youth stands for inexperience, lack of discernment, and hasty judgment.

> ***A motion-picture writer in Hollywood told me that he had to write scripts that would cater to the twelve-year-old mind.***

I can keep up with the best of them

I am now thinking of a man 65 years of age who is trying frantically to keep young. He swims with young men every Sunday, goes on long hikes, plays tennis, and boasts of his prowess and physical powers, saying, "Look, I can keep up with the best of them!"

He should remember the great truth: As a man thinketh in his heart, so is he. Your thoughts makes you what you are

Diets, exercises, and games of all kinds will not keep this man young. It is necessary for him to observe that he grows old or remains young in accordance with his processes of thinking. Your subconscious mind is conditioned by your thoughts. If your thoughts are constantly on the beautiful, the noble, and the good, you will remain young regardless of the chronological years.

He should remember the great truth: As a man thinketh in his heart, so is he. Your thoughts makes you what you are

Old Age Year

There are many people who fear old age and are uncertain about the future, because they anticipate mental and physical deterioration as the years advance. What they think and feel comes to pass.

You grow old when you lose interest in life, when you cease to dream, to hunger after new truths, and to search for new worlds to conquer. When your mind is open to new ideas, new interests, and when you raise the curtain and let in the sunshine and inspiration of new truths of life and the universe, you will be young and vital.

> ***You grow old when you lose interest in life, when you cease to dream, to hunger after new truths, and to search for new worlds to conquer.***

You have much to Give

If you are 65 or 95 years of age, realize you have much to give. You can help stabilize, advise, and direct the younger generation. You can give the benefit of your knowledge, your experience, and your wisdom. You can always look ahead for at all times you are gazing into infinite life. You will find that you can never cease to unveil the glories and wonders of life. Try to learn something new every moment of the day, and you will find your mind will always be young.

One Hundred and ten Years Old

> ***Some years ago while lecturing in Bombay, India, I was introduced to a man who said he was 110 years old. He had the most beautiful face I have ever seen.***

Some years ago while lecturing in Bombay, India, I was introduced to a man who said he was 110 years old. He had the most beautiful face I have ever seen. He seemed transfigured by the radiance of an inner light. There was a rare beauty in his eyes indicating he had grown old in years with gladness and with no indication that his mind had dimmed its lights.

Retirement—a New Venture Beginning

"What shall I do now that I am retired?" That person is saying in effect, "I am mentally and physically dead. My mind is bankrupt of ideas."

Be sure that your mind never retires. It must be like a parachute, which is no good unless it opens up. Be open and receptive to new ideas. I have seen men of 65 and 70 retire. They seemed to rot away, and in a few months passed on. They obviously felt that life was at an end.

Retirement can be a new venture, a new challenge, a new path, and the beginning of the fulfillment of a long dream. It is inexpressibly depressing to hear someone say, "What shall I do now that I am retired?" That person is saying in effect, "I am mentally and physically dead. My mind is bankrupt of ideas."

All this is a false picture. The real truth

is that you can accomplish more at 90 than you did at 60, because each day you are growing in wisdom and understanding of life and the universe through your new studies and interest.

He Upgraded to a Better Job

> ***An executive, who lives near me, was forced to retire a few months ago because he had reached the age of 65. He said to me, "I look upon my retirement as promotion from kinder¬garten to the first grade."***

An executive, who lives near me, was forced to retire a few months ago because he had reached the age of 65. He said to me, "I look upon my retirement as promotion from kinder¬garten to the first grade." He philosophized in this manner: He said that when he left high school, he went up the ladder by going to college. He realized this was a step forward in his education and understanding of life in general. Likewise, he added, now he could do the things he had always wanted to do, and therefore, his retirement was still another step forward on the ladder of life and wisdom.

He came to the wise conclusion that he was no longer going to concentrate on making a living. Now he was going to give all his attention to living life. He is an amateur photographer, and he took additional courses on the subject. He took a trip around the world and took movies of famous places. He now lectures before various groups, lodges, and clubs, and is in popular demand.

He came to the wise conclusion that he was no longer going to concentrate on making a living. Now he was going to give all his attention to living life.

There are countless ways of taking an interest in something worthwhile outside yourself. Become enthusiastic over new creative ideas, make spiritual progress, and continue to learn and to grow. In this manner you remain young in heart, because you are hungering and thirsting after new truths, and your body will reflect your thinking at all times.

Society Should not Imprism You

> ***The newspapers are taking cognizance of the fact that the voting population of the elderly in California elections is increasing by leaps and bounds.***

The newspapers are taking cognizance of the fact that the voting population of the elderly in California elections is increasing by leaps and bounds. This means that their voices will be heard in the legislature of the state and also in the halls of Con¬gress. I believe there will be enacted a federal law prohibiting employers from discrimination against men and women because of age. (note: Congress passed an age discrimination act in 1967)

A 65 year-old may be younger mentally, physically, and physiologically than many 30 year-olds. It is stupid and ridiculous refuse to hire people because they are over 40. It is like saying that they are ready for the scrap heap or the junk pile.

A 65 year-old may be younger mentally, physically, and physiologically than many 30 year-olds. It is stupid and ridiculous refuse to hire people because they are over 40.

Government treasuries at county, state, and federal levels must sustain people who are prevented from working because of age. The many organizations that refuse to hire them and benefit from their wisdom and experience will be taxed to support them. This is a form of financial suicide.

We are here to enjoy the fruit of our labor,

and to be producers and not prisoners of society which compels us to idleness. Our body slows down gradually as we advances through the years, but our conscious mind can be made much more active, alert, alive, and quickened by the inspiration from our subconscious mind. The mind, in reality, never grows old. [Job said, *"Oh that I were as in months past, as in the days when God preserved me; When His candle shined upon my head, and when by His light I walked through darkness; As I was in the days of my youth, when the secret of God was upon my tabernacle.* (Job 29:2-4).]

Oh that I were as in months past, as in the days when God preserved me; When His candle shined upon my head, and when by His light I walked through darkness...

Secret of Being Young

You can bubble over with enthusiasm and joy, as in the days of your youth, for the simple reason that you can always mentally and emotionally recapture the joyous state.

To recapture the days of your youth, feel the miraculous, healing, self-renewing power of your subconscious mind moving through your whole being. Know and feel that you are inspired, lifted up, rejuvenated, revitalized, and recharged spiritually. You can bubble over with enthusiasm and joy, as in the days of your youth, for the simple reason that you can always mentally and emotionally recapture the joyous state.

The candle that shines upon your head is divine intelligence, and reveals to you everything you need to know; it enables you to affirm the presence of your good, regardless of appearances. You walk by the guidance of your subconscious mind, because you know that the dawn appears and the shadows flee away.

Be a Visionary

> ***Instead of saying, "I am old," say, "I am wise in the way of the Divine Life." Don't let the corporation, newspapers, or statistics hold a picture before you of old age, declining years, decrepitude, senility, and uselessness.***

Instead of saying, "I am old," say, "I am wise in the way of the Divine Life." Don't let the corporation, newspapers, or statistics hold a picture before you of old age, declining years, decrepitude, senility, and uselessness. Reject it, for it is a lie. Refuse to be hypnotized by such propaganda. Affirm life—not death. Get a vision of yourself as happy, radiant, successful, serene, and powerful.

Mind Remains Young

Former President Herbert Hoover, at 88 years old, was very active and was performing monumental work. I interviewed him in his suite at the Waldorf-Astoria, New York City. I found him healthy, happy, vigorous, and full of life and enthusiasm. He was keeping several secretaries busy handling his correspondence and was himself writing books of a political and historical nature. Like all great men, I found him affable, genial, amiable, loving, and most understanding.

He was keeping several secretaries busy handling his correspondence and was himself writing books of a political and historical nature.

His mental acumen and sagacity gave me the thrill of a lifetime. He is a deeply religious man, and is full of faith in God and in the triumph of the eternal truth of life.

He was subjected to a barrage of criticism and condemnation in the years of the great depression, but he weathered the storm and did not grow old in hatred, resentment, ill will, and bitterness. On the con¬trary, he went into the silence of his soul, and communing with the Divine Presence within him, he found the peace, which is the power at the heart of God.

My father learned the French language at 65 years of age, and became an authority on it at 70. He made a study of Gaelic when he was over 60, and became an acknowledged and famous teacher of the subject.

His Mind Active at Ninety-nine

My father learned the French language at 65 years of age, and became an authority on it at 70. He made a study of Gaelic when he was over 60, and became an acknowledged and famous teacher of the subject. He assisted my sister in a school of higher learning and continued to do so until he passed away at 99. His mind was as clear at 99 as it was when he was 20. Moreover, his handwriting and his reasoning powers had improved with age. Truly, you are as old as you think and feel.

Our Senior Citizens are Important

Marcus Porcius Cato, the Roman patriot, learned Greek at 80. Madame Ernestine Schumann-Heink, the great German-American contralto, reached the pinnacle of her musical success after she became a grandmother. It is wonderful to behold the accomplishments of the oldsters. General Douglas MacArthur, Harry S. Truman, General Dwight David

Madame Ernestine Schumann-Heink, the great German-American contralto, reached the pinnacle of her musical success after she became a grandmother.

Eisenhower, and American financier Bernard Baruch were interesting, active, and contributing their talents and wisdom to the world in their senior years.

The Greek philosopher, Socrates, learned to play musical instruments when he was 80 years old. Michelangelo was painting his greatest canvases at 80. At 80, Cios Simonides won the prize for poetry, Johann von Goethe finished Faust, and Leopold von Ranke commenced his *History of the World*, which he finished at 92.

The Greek philosopher, Socrates, learned to play musical instruments when he was 80 years old. Michelangelo was painting his greatest canvases at 80.

Alfred Tennyson wrote a magnificent poem, "Crossing the Bar," at 83. Isaac Newton was hard at work close to 85. At 88 John Wesley was directing, preaching, and guiding Methodism. We have several men of 95 years who come to my lectures, and they tell me they are in better health now than they were at 20. Let us place our senior citizens in high places and give them every opportunity to bring forth the flowers of Paradise.

If you are retired, get interested in the laws of life and the wonders of your subconscious mind. Do something you have always wanted to do. Study new subjects, and investigate new ideas.

If you are retired, get interested in the laws of life and the wonders of your subconscious mind. Do something you have always wanted to do. Study new subjects, and investigate new ideas.

Pray as follows: *"As the deer pants for streams of water, so my soul pants for you, my God.* (Psalms 42:1).

Benefits of Old Age

Old age really means the contemplation of the truths of God from the highest standpoint. Realize that you are on an endless journey, a series of important steps in the ceaseless, tireless, endless ocean of life.

"But the fruit of the Spirit is love, joy, peace, patience, gentleness, goodness, faith, meekness, temperance: against such there is no law."

You are a son of Infinite Life, which knows no end, and you are a child of Eternity.

3

Miracles of Healing

There is only one healing power. It is called by many names, such as God, Infinite Healing Presence, Nature, Divine Love, Divine Providence, the Miraculous Healing Power, Life, Life Principle, as well as many others. This knowledge goes back into the dim recesses of the past. An inscription has been found written over ancient an temple which reads: "The doctor dresses the wound, and God heals the patient."

The healing presence of God is within you. No psychologist, minister, doctor, surgeon, priest, or psychiatrist heals anyone. For example, the surgeon removes a tumor, thereby removing the block and making way for the healing power of God to restore you. The psychologist or psychiatrist endeavors to remove the mental block and encourages the patient to adopt a new mental attitude which tends to release the Healing Presence, flowing through the patient as harmony, health, and peace. The minister asks you to forgive yourself and others and to get in tune with the Infinite by letting the healing power of love, peace, and good will flow through your subconscious mind, thereby cleansing all the negative patterns that may be lodged there.

The healing presence of God is within you. No psychologist, minister, doctor, surgeon, priest, or psychiatrist heals anyone.

This miraculous healing power in your

subconscious mind, if scientifically directed, can heal your mind, body, and affairs of all disease and impediments. This healing power will respond to you regardless of your race, creed, or color. It does not care whether you belong to any church or whether you have any creedal affiliations or not. You have had hundreds of healings since you were a child. You can recall how this healing presence brought curative results to cuts, bums, bruises, contusions, sprains, etc., and, in all probability, like the author, you did not aid the healing in any way by the application of external remedies.

You have had hundreds of healings since you were a child. You can recall how this healing presence brought curative results to cuts, bums, bruises, contusions, sprains, etc.

Spiritual Healing-Voice

A few years ago a young man from a local university came to see me with the complaint that he was constantly hearing spirit-voices, that they made him do nasty things, and that they would not let him alone; neither would they permit him to read the Bible or other spiritual books. He was convinced that he was talking to supernatural beings.

> ***This young man was clairaudient, and, not knowing that all men possess this faculty to some degree, he began to think it was due to evil spirits.***

This young man was clairaudient, and, not knowing that all men possess this faculty to some degree, he began to think it was due to evil spirits. His superstitious beliefs caused him to ascribe it to departed spirits. Through constant worry, he became a monomaniac on the subject. His subconscious mind, dominated and controlled by an all-potent but false suggestion, gradually took over control and mastery of his objective faculties, and his reason abdicated its throne. He was what you would call mentally unbalanced, as are all men who allow their false beliefs to obtain the ascendancy.

> ***I explained to this university student that his subconscious mind is of tremendous importance and significance and that it can be influenced negatively and positively...***

I explained to this university student that his subconscious mind is of tremendous importance and significance and that it can be influenced negatively and positively, but he had to make sure that he influenced it only positively, constructively, and harmoniously. The subconscious mind possesses transcendent powers, but it is at the same time amenable to good and bad suggestions. The explanation which I gave him made a profound impression on him.

I gave him the following written prayer which he was to repeat for ten or fifteen minutes three or four times a day:

God's love, peace, harmony, and wisdom flood my mind and heart. I love the truth, I hear the truth, and I know the truth that God is Love, and His love surrounds me, enfolds me, and enwraps me. God's river of peace floods my mind, and I give thanks for my freedom.

God's love, peace, harmony, and wisdom flood my mind and heart. I love the truth, I hear the truth, and I know the truth that God is Love...

He repeated this prayer slowly, quietly, reverently, and with deep feeling, particularly prior to sleep. By identifying himself with harmony and peace, he brought about a rearrangement of the thought- patterns and imagery of his mind, and a healing followed. He brought about a healing of his mind by repetition of these truths, coupled with faith and expectancy.

My own prayer for him night and morning was as follows: "John is thinking rightly. He is reflecting Divine wisdom and Divine intelligence in all his ways. His mind is the perfect mind of God, unchanging and eternal. He hears the voice of God, which is the inner voice of peace and love. God's river of peace governs his mind, and he is full of wisdom, poise, balance, and understanding. Whatever is vexing him is leaving him now, and I pronounce him free and at peace."

John is thinking rightly. He is reflecting Divine wisdom and Divine intelligence in all his ways. His mind is the perfect mind of God, unchanging and eternal.

I meditated on these truths night and morning, getting the "feel" of peace and harmony; at the end of a week this young man was completely free and at peace.

Death was Inevitable

> ***Some time ago, a woman told me that her child had a very high fever and was not expected to live. The doctor had prescribed small doses of aspirin and had administered an antibiotic preparation.***

Some time ago, a woman told me that her child had a very high fever and was not expected to live. The doctor had prescribed small doses of aspirin and had administered an antibiotic preparation. The mother, who was involved in a contemplated divorce action, was terribly agitated and emotionally disturbed. This disturbed feeling was communicated subconsciously to the child, and naturally, the child got Children are at the mercy of their parents and are controlled by the dominant mental atmosphere and emotional climate of those around them. They have not yet reached the age of reason when they can take control of their own thoughts, emotions, and reactions to life.

The mother, at my suggestion, decided to become more at ease and relax her tensions by reading the 23rd Psalm, praying for guidance and for the peace and harmony of her husband. She poured out love and good will to him and overcame her resentment and inner rage. The fever of the child was due to the suppressed rage and anger of the mother, which was subjectively felt by the child and expressed as a high fever due to the excitation of the child's mind.

The mother, at my suggestion, decided to become more at ease and relax her tensions by reading the 23rd Psalm, praying for guidance and for the peace and harmony of her husband.

Having quieted her own mind, the mother

began to pray for her child in this manner: "Spirit, which is God, is the life of my child. Spirit has no temperature; It is never sick or feverish. The peace of God flows through my child's mind and body. The harmony, health, love, and perfection of God are made manifest in every atom of my child's body now. She is relaxed and at ease, poised, serene, and calm. I am now stirring up the gift of God within her, and all is well."

She repeated the above prayer every hour for several hours. Shortly thereafter, she noticed a remarkable change in her child, who awakened and asked for a doll and something to eat.

She repeated the above prayer every hour for several hours. Shortly thereafter, she noticed a remarkable change in her child, who awakened and asked for a doll and something to eat. The temperature became normal. What had happened?

The fever left the little girl because the mother was no longer feverish or agitated in her mind. Her mood of peace, harmony, and love was instantaneously felt by the child, and a corresponding reaction was produced.

Healing Presence is Within US

We are all "natural-born healers" for the simple reason that the healing presence of God is within all men, and all of us can contact It with our thoughts. It responds to all. This Healing Presence is in the dog, the cat, the tree, and the bird. It is omnipresent and is the life of all things.

We are all "natural-born healers" for the simple reason that the healing presence of God is within all men, and all of us can contact It with our thoughts.

Amount of Faith

There are different degrees of faith. There is the man who, through faith, heals his ulcers, and another who heals a deep-seated, so-called incurable malignancy. It is as easy for the healing presence of God to heal a tubercular lung as it is to heal a Cut on your finger. There is no great or small in the God that made us all; there is no big or little, no hard or easy. Omnipotence is within all men. The prayers of the man who lays his hand on another in order to induce a healing simply appeal to the cooperation of the patient's unconscious, whether the latter knows it or not, or whether he ascribes it to Divine intercession or not, and a response takes place; for according to the patient's faith is it done unto him.

> ***There are different degrees of faith. There is the man who, through faith, heals his ulcers, and another who heals a deep-seated, so-called incurable malignancy.***

Story of the Man with Palsy

An old friend of mine in New York City suffered from palsy and tremors some years ago. His legs would become locked so that inability to move was experienced. Panic would ensue, and my friend would be frozen to the spot, even in the middle of a busy street. He got some mild relief from sedatives and antispasmodics which were prescribed by his physician; however, this condition of constant fear, panic, and foreboding was wearing him down. The following procedure was adopted.

An old friend of mine in New York City suffered from palsy and tremors some years ago. His legs would become locked so that inability to move was experienced.

The first step was to get him to see that there was a miraculous healing power within him which had made his body and which also could heal it. I suggested to him that he read the 5th Chapter of Luke, verses 18¬24, and a related passage, Mark 2:3-5, where Jesus said to the man with the palsy: *'Man, thy sins are forgiven thee . . . I say unto thee, Arise, and take thy couch, and go into thine house."*

He read these verses avidly and was deeply moved by them. I explained to him that the couch or bed mentioned in the Bible means the bed in which a man lies in his own mind.

He read these verses avidly and was deeply moved by them. I explained to him that the couch or bed mentioned in the Bible means the bed in which a man lies in his own mind. The paralyzed man in the Bible undoubtedly was lying down amidst the thoughts of fear, doubt, condemnation, guilt, and superstition. These thoughts paralyze the mind and body.

We are told that Jesus healed the man of palsy by forgiving him his sins. To sin is to miss the mark, the goal of health, happiness, and peace. You forgive yourself by identifying mentally and emotionally with your ideal and continuing to do so until it gets within you as a conviction or subjective embodiment. You are sinning also when you think negatively or if you resent, hate, condemn, or engage in fear or worry. You are always sinning when you deviate or run away from your announced goal or aim in life, which should always be peace, harmony, wisdom, and perfect health - the life more abundant.

My friend admitted to me that he was full of hatred toward a brother who had double-crossed him years ago in a financial deal.

My friend admitted to me that he was full of hatred toward a brother who had double-crossed him years ago in a financial deal. He also was full of guilt and self-condemnation and he realized that, like the paralytic in the Bible, he could not be healed until his sins had been cancelled by simply forgiving himself and his brother. He admitted to himself that his physical condition was quite a problem, but that he didn't have to have it.

He turned to the healing presence of God within him and affirmed boldly:

I fully and freely forgive myself for harboring negative and destructive thoughts, and I resolve to purify my mind from now on.

"I fully and freely forgive myself for harboring negative and destructive thoughts, and I resolve to purify my mind from now on. I surrender and release my brother to God, and wherever he is, I sincerely wish for him health, happiness, and all the blessing of God. I am now aligned with the Infinite Healing Power, and I feel Divine love flowing through every atom of my being. I know that God's love is now permeating and saturating my whole body, making me whole and perfect. I sense the peace that passeth understanding. My body is a temple of the living God, and God is in His holy temple and I am free. As he meditated on these truths, he gradually became reconditioned to health and harmony. As he changed his mind, he changed his body. Changed attitudes change everything. Today he walks joyously and freely, completely healed."

An irate young man came to interview me, stating that his boss had fired him and had said to him, "You're like the man in the Bible with the withered hand."

The Healing of the Withered Hand

An irate young man came to interview me, stating that his boss had fired him and had said to him, "You're like the man in the Bible with the withered hand." He said to me, "What did he mean? My hands are all right, they are perfectly normal." My explanation was as follows: In the correct interpretation of the Bible, it must be understood that principles are personified as persons in order to make portrayal and interaction vivid and forceful. We must not confine the story of the man with the withered hand to its literal meaning. The hand is a symbol of power, direction, and effectiveness. With your hand, you fashion, mold, direct, and design. Symbolically, a man has a withered hand when he has an inferiority complex and feels guilty and inadequate, or is a defeatist. Such a man does not function efficiently and is not expressing his God-given powers.

My explanation was as follows: In the correct interpretation of the Bible, it must be understood that principles are personified as persons in order to make portrayal and interaction vivid and forceful.

This young man admitted that his dreams, ambitions, ideals, plans, and purposes were withered and frozen in his mind because he did not know how to bring them to pass. Not knowing the laws of mind and how to pray correctly, he found that his wonderful ideas died a¬borning in his mind, resulting in frustration and neurosis. He was stagnating, literally dying on the vine. Furthermore, he was demoting and depreciating himself. His attitude toward life was all wrong; moreover, he admitted that his work was shoddy and desultory.

This young man admitted that his dreams, ambitions, ideals, plans, and purposes were withered and frozen in his mind because he did not know how to bring them to pass.

His hand (his ability to achieve and to accomplish) withered by saying to himself, "If I had Joe's brains or his wealth . . . his connections . . . I could advance and be somebody. But look at me, just a nobody. I was born on the wrong side of the tracks. I must he satisfied with my lot. I have a withered hand."

A remarkable change took place in this man, however, when he decided to stretch forth his hand by enlarging his concept and estimate of himself.

A remarkable change took place in this man, however, when he decided to stretch forth his hand by enlarging his concept and estimate of himself. He formed a picture in his mind of what he wished to achieve, i.e., to direct a large organization and to be successful. He began to affirm frequently, "I can do all things, through the God- power which strengthens, guides, controls, and directs me. I realize that I am going where my vision is. I now turn with faith and confidence to the Infinite Intelligence within me, knowing that I am directed by an inner wisdom. I know in my heart that the God-power flows through the patterns of thought and imagery in my mind, and I am under a Divine compulsion to succeed."

As he identified himself mentally and emotionally with these new concepts, he went forward from promotion to promotion and is now general manager of a large corporation, his current salary exceeding $75,000 annually.

As he identified himself mentally and emotionally with these new concepts, he went forward from promotion to promotion and is now general manager of a large corporation, his current salary exceeding $75,000 annually.

The Way the Hopeless Case Healed

When it says the dead man sat up and began to speak, it means that when your prayer is answered you speak in a new tongue of joyous health, and you exude an inner radiance. Your dead hopes and desires speak when you bear witness to your inner beliefs and assumptions.

As a corollary to this, I would like to tell about a young man I saw in Ireland a few years ago. He is a distant relative. He was in a comatose condition; his kidneys had not functioned for three days. His condition had been pronounced hopeless when I went to see him, accompanied by one of his brothers. I knew that he was very religious, and I said to him, "God is right here, and you see him. He is putting his hand out and is this moment laying his hand upon you."

As a corollary to this, I would like to tell about a young man I saw in Ireland a few years ago. He is a distant relative. He was in a comatose condition...

I repeated this several times, slowly, gently, and positively. He was unconscious when I spoke and was not consciously aware of either of us. He sat up in bed, however, opened his eyes, and said to both of us, "God was here; I know I am healed I shall live."

What had happened? This man's subconscious mind had accepted my statement that God was there, and his subconscious projected that thought-form, i.e.

What had happened? This man's subconscious mind had accepted my statement that God was there, and his subconscious projected that thought-form, i.e. this man's concept of God was portrayed based on what he saw in religious places in statues, paintings, etc. He believed that God was there in the flesh and that he had placed his hands upon him.

The readers of my book, The Power of Your Subconscious Mind, are well aware of the fact that you can tell a man who is in a trance that his grandfather is here now and that he will see him clearly. He will see what he believes to be his grandfather. His subconscious reveals the image of his grandfather based on his subconscious memory picture. You can give the same man a post-hypnotic suggestion by sayingto him, "When you come out of this trance, you will greet your grandfather and talk to him," and he will do exactly that. This is called a subjective hallucination.

> ***The faith which was kindled in the unconscious of my religious relative, based on his firm belief that God came to heal him, was the healing factor.***

The faith which was kindled in the unconscious of my religious relative, based on his *firm belief* that God came to heal him, was the healing factor. It is always done unto us according to our faith, mental conviction, or just blind belief. His subconscious mind was amenable to my suggestion; his deeper mind received and acted upon the idea I had implanted in his mind. In a sense, you could call such an incident the resurrection of the dead. It was the resurrection of his health and vitality. According to his belief was it done unto him.

Blind Faith and True Faith

True faith is based on the knowledge of the way your conscious and subconscious minds function and on the combined harmonious functioning of these two levels of mind scientifically directed. Blind faith is healing without any scientific understanding whatsoever of the forces involved. The voodoo doctor or witch doctor in the jungles of Africa heals by faith, and so do the bones

True faith is based on the knowledge of the way your conscious and subconscious minds function and on the combined harmonious functioning of these two levels of mind scientifically directed.

of dogs (believed to be the bones of saints by the believer), or anything else which moves man's mind from fear to faith.

In all instances - regardless of the technique, *modus operandi* process, incantation, or invocation offered to saints and spirits - it is the subconscious mind that does the healing. Whatever you believe is operative instantly in your subconscious mind.

Be like the little eight-year-old boy in our Sunday school. Eye drops were not clearing up his eye infection, and he prayed as follows: "God, you made my eyes. I demand action, I want healing now. Hurry up. Thank you."

Be like the little eight-year-old boy in our Sunday school. Eye drops were not clearing up his eye infection, and he prayed as follows: "God, you made my eyes. I demand action, I want healing now. Hurry up. Thank you." He had a remarkable healing because of his simplicity, spontaneity, and childlike faith in God.

Process of Spiritual Treatment

Spiritual treatment means that you turn to the Indwelling God and remind yourself of His peace, harmony, wholeness, beauty, boundless love, and limitless power. Know that God loves you and cares for you. As you pray this way the fear gradually will fade away. If you pray about a heart condition, do not think of the organ as diseased as this would not be spiritual thinking. Thoughts are things. Your spiritual thought takes the form of cells, tissues, nerves, and organs. To think of a damaged heart or high blood pressure tends to suggest more of what you already

> ***Spiritual treatment means that you turn to the Indwelling God and remind yourself of His peace, harmony, wholeness, beauty, boundless love, and limitless power.***

have. Cease dwelling on symptoms, organs or any part of the body. Turn your mind to God and His love. Feel and know that there is only one healing Presence and Power, and to its corollary: There is no Power to challenge the action of God.

Quietly and lovingly affirm that the uplifting, healing, strengthening power of the healing Presence is flowing through you making you every whit whole. Know and feel that the harmony, beauty, and life of God manifest themselves in you as strength, peace, vitality, wholeness, and right action. Get a clear realization of this, and the damaged heart or other disease organ will be cured in the light of God's love.

> ***Feel and know that there is only one healing Presence and Power, and to its corollary: There is no Power to challenge the action of God.***

As mentioned in holy books, Glorify God your in body.

Important Points

1. The healing power of God is within you. Remove any mental block and let the healing power flow through you.

2. A monomaniac is a man who permits his mind to be dominated and controlled by an all-potent but false suggestion.

> ***When a mother is agitated and seething with inner turmoil and rage, this negative emotion is communicated to the subconscious of her child and can cause fever.***

3. When a mother is agitated and seething with inner turmoil and rage, this negative emotion is communicated to the subconscious of her child and can cause fever. Let God's river of peace flood the mind

and heart, and the child's fever will abate and harmony will be restored.

4. All of us are natural-born healers because the Infinite Healing Presence is within us, and we can contact It with our thoughts and beliefs.

5. The miraculous healing power which made your body knows how to heal it. It knows all the processes and functions of your body. Trust the healing power, and accept a healing now.

6. You can recondition yourself to health and harmony as you meditate frequently on harmony, vitality, wholeness, beauty, and perfection.

7. In the Bible, principles are personified as persons in order to make portrayal and interaction vivid and forceful. You can overcome a feeling of inferiority by joining up with God

and by sensing that one with God is a majority.

8. There are no incurable diseases. There are incurable people who believe they can't be healed, and according to their belief is it done unto them.

9. Faith healing is healing without any scientific understanding of the forces involved. Spiritual mind healing is the combined and harmonious functioning of your conscious and subconscious mind, scientifically directed for a specific purpose. In all instances, it is the subconscious mind that heals regardless of the technique or process used.

Facing the Word Incurable

Don't let the word "incurable" frighten you. Realize that you are dealing with the Creative Intelligence which made your body and that, although some men will say that a healing is impossible, be assured that this infinite Healing Presence is instantly available, and you can always draw on its power through the creative law of your own mind. Make use of this power now and perform miracles in your life. Remember that a miracle cannot prove that which is impossible; it is a confirmation of that which is possible, for . . . with God all things are possible."

The word "Lord" in the Bible means the creative law of your mind. There is a deep-lying, healing principle which permeates the entire universe, that flows through your mental patterns...

The word "Lord" in the Bible means the creative law of your mind. There is a deep-lying, healing principle which permeates the entire universe, that flows through your mental patterns, images, and choices, and objectifies them in form. You can bring into your life anything you wish through this infinite healing principle which operates through your own mind.

You may use this universal healing principle for any particular purpose. It is not confined to healing of the mind or body. It is the same principle which attracts to you the ideal husband or wife, prospers you in business, finds for you your true place in life, and reveals answers to your most difficult problems. Through the correct application of this principle, you can become a great salesman, musician, physician, or surgeon. You can use it to bring harmony where discord exists, peace to supplant pain, joy in place of sadness, and abundance in place of poverty.

You may use this universal healing principle for any particular purpose. It is not confined to healing of the mind or body.

Healing of Dropsy

I knew a man in London, England, who was not only very religious but was completely free from any ill will or resentment. However, he saw his father die of dropsy, and it made a very deep and lasting impression on him; he told me that all his life since that event he feared that the same thing would happen to him. He also told me that his father by way of treatment used to be tapped with an instrument, and that the doctor would draw out large amounts of water from his abdominal area. This lingering fear, which was never neutralized, was undoubtedly the cause of his dropsical condition. He did not know the simple psychological truth which Dr. Phineas Parkhurst Quimby of Maine had elucidated about one hundred years ago. Dr. Quimby said that if you believe something,

> ***I knew a man in London, England, who was not only very religious but was completely free from any ill will or resentment.***

it will manifest, whether you are consciously thinking of it or not. This man's fear grew into a conviction that he would become a victim of the same disorder that had troubled his father. This explanation, however, helped the man considerably. He began o realize that he had accepted a lie as truth.

I pointed out to him that his fear was a perversion of the truth, a fear which had no real power because there is no principle behind disease. There is a principle of health, none of disease; a principle of abundance, none of poverty; a principal of honesty, none of deceit; a principle of mathematics, none of error; and a principle of beauty, none of ugliness. Fortunately, his belief was in the only power which controlled him, and he knew that his mind could be used negatively or positively.

I pointed out to him that his fear was a perversion of the truth, a fear which had no real power because there is no principle behind disease.

He came to a definite conclusion in his mind by reasoning that the Healing Presence which made him was still with him and that his disease was due to a disordered group of disease soaked thoughts; thus he rearranged his mind to conform to the Divine pattern of harmony, health, and wholeness.

The Healing Presence is now going to work, transforming, healing, restoring, and controlling all processes of my body according to Its wisdom and Divine nature.

Before going to sleep at night, he would affirm with feeling and with deep meaning behind each word: "The Healing Presence is now going to work, transforming, healing, restoring, and controlling all processes of my body according to Its wisdom and Divine nature. My entire system is cleansed, purified, and quickened by the vitalizing energy of God. Divine circulation, assimilation, and elimination operate in my mind and body. The joy of the Lord is my abiding strength. I am made every whit whole, and I give thanks."

He repeated this prayer every night for about thirty days. At the end of that time, his mind had reached a conviction of health, and his physician dismissed him as whole and perfect.

He repeated this prayer every night for about thirty days. At the end of that time, his mind had reached a conviction of health, and his physician dismissed him as whole and perfect.

Healing Process

The first step in healing is not to be afraid of the manifest condition from this very moment. The second step is to realize that the condition is only the product of past thinking, which will have no more power to continue its existence. The third step is mentally to exalt the miraculous healing power of God within you.

This procedure instantly will stop the production of all mental poisons in you or in the person for whom you are praying. Live in the embodiment of your desire, and your thought and feeling will soon be made manifest. Do not allow yourself to be swayed by human opinion and worldly fears, but live emotionally in the belief that it is God in action in your mind and body.

> ***This procedure instantly will stop the production of all mental poisons in you or in the person for whom you are praying. Live in the embodiment of your desire...***

Spiritual Blindness

Millions of people are "blind," i.e., they are psychological and spiritually "blind" because they do not know that they become what they think all day long. Man is spiritually and mentally "blind" when he is hateful, resentful, or envious of others. He does not know that he is actually secreting mental poisons which tend to destroy him.

Thousands of people are constantly saying that there is no way to solve their problems, and their situation is hopeless. Such an attitude is the result of spiritual blindness. Man begins to see spiritually and mentally when he gets a new understanding of his mental powers, and develops a conscious awareness that the wisdom and intelligence in his subconscious can solve all his problems.

Thousands of people are constantly saying that there is no way to solve their problems, and their situation is hopeless. Such an attitude is the result of spiritual blindness.

Everyone should become aware of the inter-relationship and interaction of the conscious and subconscious mind. Persons who were once blind to these truths, after careful introspection, will now begin to see the vision of health, wealth, happiness, and peace of mind that can be theirs through the correct application of the laws of mind.

Vision-Its eternal and Indestructible

> ***We do not create vision, rather we manifest or release it. We see through the eye, not with it. The cornea of the eye is stimulated by light waves from objects in space...***

We do not create vision, rather we manifest or release it. We see through the eye, not with it. The cornea of the eye is stimulated by light waves from objects in space; through the optic nerve, these stimuli are carried to the brain. When the inner light, or intelligence, meets the outer light in this manner, by a process of interpretation, we see.

Your eyes symbolize Divine love and a delight in the ways of God, plus a hunger and thirst for God's truth. Your right eye symbolizes right thought and right action. The left eye symbolizes God's love and wisdom. Think right and radiate good will to all, and you will focus perfectly.

Special Prayer for Eyes and Ears

I am the Lord that health me. My vision is spiritual, eternal, and a quality of my consciousness. My eyes are Divine ideas, and they are always functioning perfectly.

I am the Lord that health me. My vision is spiritual, eternal, and a quality of my consciousness. My eyes are Divine ideas, and they are always functioning perfectly.

My perception of spiritual Truth is clear and powerful. The light of understanding dawns in me; I see more and more of God's Truth every day. I see spiritually; I see mentally; I see physically. I see images of Truth and Beauty everywhere.

The infinite Healing Presence is now, this moment, rebuilding my eyes. They are perfect, Divine instruments, enabling me to receive messages from the world within and the world without. The glory of God is revealed in my eyes.

The infinite Healing Presence is now, this moment, rebuilding my eyes. They are perfect, Divine instruments, enabling me to receive messages from the world within and the world without.

I hear the Truth; I love the Truth; I know the Truth. My ears are God's perfect ideas, functioning perfectly at all times. My ears are the perfect instruments which reveal God's harmony to me. The love, beauty, and harmony of God flow through my eyes and ears; I am in tune with the Infinite. I hear the still, small voice of God within me. The Holy Spirit quickens my hearing, and my ears are open and free.

Steps Towards Healing

1. Man says it's impossible, but with God all things are possible. You can be healed by God, Who created you.

2. The healing principle flows through your mental patterns of thought and imagery, bringing all things you wish into manifestation.

3. If you believe something, it will be manifest -- whether or not you are consciously thinking of it. Believe only in that which heals, blesses, and inspires you.

4. Exalt the power of God in the midst of you, and you will stop the spread of any disease in your body.

5. The thankful heart is close to God. Let all your prayers be made known with praise and thanksgiving.

6. You are spiritually blind when you

don't know that thoughts are things, that what you feel you attract, and that what you imagine, you become.

7. Vision is spiritual, eternal, and indestructible. A wonderful prayer for the eyes is to affirm regularly: "I see better spiritually, mentally, and physically."

8. "*I* will lift up mine eyes unto the hills, from whence cometh my help."

About the Author

Joseph Murphy was born on May 20, 1898, in a small town in the County of Cork, Ireland. His father, Denis Murphy, was a deacon and professor at t-he National School of Ireland, a Jesuit facility. His mother, Ellen, née Connelly, was a housewife, who later gave birth to another son, John, and a daughter, Catherine.

Joseph was brought up in a strict Catholic household. His father was quite devout and, indeed, was one of the few lay professors who taught Jesuit seminarians. He had a broad knowledge of many subjects and developed in his son the desire to study and learn.

Ireland at that time was suffering from one of its many economic depressions, and many families were starving. Although Denis Murphy was steadily employed, his income was barely enough to sustain the family.

Young Joseph was enrolled in the National School and was a brilliant student. He was encouraged to study for the priesthood and was accepted as a Jesuit seminarian. However, by the time he reached his late teen years, he began to question the Catholic orthodoxy of the Jesuits, and he withdrew from the seminary. Since his goal was to explore new ideas and gain new experiences—a goal he could not pursue in Catholic-dominated Ireland—he left his family to go to America.

He arrived at the Ellis Island Immigration Center with only $5 in his pocket. His first project was to find a place to live. He was fortunate to locate a rooming house where he shared a room with a pharmacist who worked in local drugstore.

Joseph's knowledge of English was minimal, as Gaelic was spoken both in his home and at school, so like most Irish immigrants, Joseph worked as a day laborer, earning enough to keep fed and housed.

He and his roommate became good friends, and when a job opened up at the drugstore where his friend worked, he was hired to be an assistant to the pharmacist. He immediately enrolled in a school to study pharmacy. With his keen mind and desire to learn, it didn't take long before Joseph passed the qualification exams and became a full-fledged pharmacist. He now made enough money to rent his own apartment. After a few years, he purchased the drugstore, and for the next few years ran a successful business.

When the United States entered World War II, Joseph enlisted in the Army and was assigned to work as a pharmacist in the medical unit of the 88th Infantry Division. At that time, he renewed his interest in religion and began to read extensively about various religious beliefs. After his discharge from the Army, he chose not to return to his career in pharmacy. He traveled extensively, taking courses in several universities both in the United States and abroad.

From his studies, Joseph became enraptured by the various Asian religions and went to India to learn about them in depth. He studied all of the major religions from the time of their beginning. He extended these studies to the great philosophers from ancient times until the present.

Although he studied with some of the most intelligent and far-sighted professors, the one person who most influenced Joseph was Dr. Thomas Troward, who was a judge as well as a philosopher, doctor, and professor. Judge Troward became Joseph's mentor.

From him he not only learned philosophy, theology, and law, but also was introduced to mysticism and particularly, the Masonic order. He became an active member of this order and over the years rose in the Masonic ranks to the 32nd degree in the Scottish Rite.

Upon his return to the United States, Joseph chose to become a minister and bring his broad knowledge to the public. As his concept of Christianity was not traditional and indeed ran counter to most of the Christian denominations, he founded his own church in Los Angeles. He attracted a small number of congregants, but it did not take long for his message of optimism and hope rather than the “sin and damnation” sermons of so many ministers to attract many men and women to his church.

Dr. Joseph Murphy was a proponent of the New Thought movement. This movement was developed in the late 19th and early 20th centuries by many philosophers and deep thinkers who studied this phenomenon and preached, wrote, and practiced a new way of looking at life. By combining a metaphysical, spiritual, and pragmatic approach to the way we think and live, they uncovered the secret of attaining what we truly desire.

The proponents of the New Thought movement preached a new idea of life that brings out new methods and more perfected results, and we have the power to use it to enrich our lives. We can do all these things only as we have found the law and worked out the understanding of the law, which God seemed to have written in riddles in the past.

Of course, Dr. Murphy wasn't the only minister to preach this positive message. Several churches, whose ministers and congregants were influenced by the New Thought movement, were founded and developed in the decades following World War II. The Church of Religious Science, the Unity Church, and similar places of worship preach philosophies similar to this.

Dr. Murphy named his organization The Church of Divine Science. He often shared platforms, conducted joint programs with his similar-thinking colleagues, and trained other men and women to join their ministry.

Over the years, other churches joined with him in developing an organization called the Federation of Divine Science, which acts an umbrella for all Divine Science churches. Each of the Divine Science church leaders continues to push for more education, and Dr. Murphy was one of the leaders to support the creation of the Divine Science School in St. Louis, Missouri, to train new ministers and provide ongoing educational education for both ministers and congregants.

The annual meeting of the Divine Science ministers was a must to attend, and Dr. Murphy was a featured speaker at them. He encouraged the participants to study and continue to learn, particularly about the importance of the subconscious mind.

Over the next few years, Murphy's local

Church of Divine Science grew so large that his building was too small to hold them. He rented The Wilshire Ebell Theater, a former movie theater. His services were so well attended that even this venue could not always accommodate all who wished to attend. Classes conducted by Dr. Murphy and his staff supplemented his Sunday services that were attended by 1,300 to 1,500 people. These were supplemented by seminars and lectures that were held most days and evenings. The church remained at the Wilshire Ebell Theater in Los Angeles until 1976, when it moved to a new location in Laguna Hills, California, near a retirement community.

To reach the vast numbers of people who wanted to hear his message, Dr. Murphy created a weekly radio talk show, which eventually reached an audience of over a million listeners.

Many of his followers wanted more than just summaries and suggested that he tape his lectures and radio programs. He was at first reluctant to do so, but agreed to experiment. His radio programs were recorded on extra-large 78rpm discs, a common practice at that time. He had six cassettes made from one of these discs and placed them on the information table in the lobby of the Wilshire Ebell Theater. They sold out the first hour. This started a new venture. His tapes of his lecture explaining biblical texts, and providing meditations and prayers for his listeners were not only sold in his church, but in other churches, bookstores, and via the mail.

As the church grew, Dr. Murphy added a staff of professional and administrative personnel to assist him in the many programs in which he was involved and in researching and preparing his first books. One of the most effective members of his staff was his administrative secretary, Dr. Jean Wright. The working relationship developed into a romance, and they were married—a lifelong partnership that enriched both of their lives.

At this time (the 1950s), there were very few major publishers of spiritually inspired material. The Murphy's located some small publishers in the Los Angeles area, and with them produced a series of small books (often 30 to 50 pages printed in pamphlet form) that were sold, mostly in churches, from $1.50 to $3.00 per book. When the orders for these books increased to the point where they required second and third printings, major publishers recognized that there was a market for such books and added them to their catalogs.

Dr. Murphy became well known outside of the Los Angeles area as a result of his books, tapes, and radio broadcasts and was invited to lecture all over the country. He did not limit his lectures to religious matters, but spoke on the historical values of life, the art of wholesome living, and on the teachings of great philosophers—both from the Western and Oriental cultures.

As Dr. Murphy never learned to drive, he had to arrange for somebody to drive him to the various places where he was invited to lecture and other places in his very busy schedule. One of Jean's functions as his administrative secretary and later as his wife was to plan

his assignments, arrange for trains or flights, airport pickups, hotel accommodations, and all the other details of the trips.

The Murphy's traveled frequently to many countries around the world. One of his favorite working vacations was to hold seminars on cruise ships. These trips were for a week or more and would take him to many countries around the world.

One of Dr. Murphy's most rewarding activities was speaking to the inmates at many prisons. Many ex-convicts wrote him over the years, telling him how his words had truly turned their lives around and inspired them to live spiritual and meaningful lives.

He toured the United States and many

countries in Europe and Asia. In his lectures, he emphasized the importance of understanding the power of the subconscious mind and the life principles based on belief in the one God, the "I AM."

Dr. Murphy's pamphlet-sized books were so popular that he began to expand them into more detailed and longer works. His wife gave us some insight into his manner and method of writing. She reported that he wrote his manuscripts on a tablet and pressed so hard on his pencil or pen that you could read the page by the imprint on the next page. He seemed to be in a trance while writing. His writing style was to remain in his office for four to six hours without disturbance until he stopped and said that was enough for the day. Each day was the same. He never went back into the office again until the next morning to finish what he'd started. He took no food or drink while he was working, He was just alone with his thoughts and his huge library of books, to which he referred from time to time. His wife sheltered him from visitors and calls and kept things moving for church business and other activities.

Dr. Murphy was always looking for a simple way to discuss the issues and to elaborate points that would explain in detail how it affects the individual. He chose some of his lectures to present on cassettes, records, or CDs, as the technologies developed and new methods entered the audio field.

His entire work of CDs and cassettes are tools that can be used for most problems that individuals encounter in life, and have been time-tested to accomplish the goals as intended. His basic theme is that the solution to problems lies within oneself. Outside elements cannot change one's thinking. That is, your mind is your own. To live a better life, it's your mind not outside circumstances that you must change. You create your own destiny. The power of change is in your mind, and by using the power of your subconscious mind, you can make those changes for the better.

Dr. Murphy wrote more than 30 books. His most famous work, The Power of the Unconscious Mind, which was first published in 1963, became an immediate bestseller. It was acclaimed as one of the best self-help guides ever written. Millions of copies have been sold and continue to be sold all over the world.

Among some of his other best-selling books were Telepsychics—The Magic Power of Perfect Living, The Amazing Laws of Cosmic Mind, Secrets of the I-Ching, The Miracle of Mind Dynamics, Your Infinite Power to Be Rich, and The Cosmic Power Within You.

Dr. Murphy died in December 1981, and his wife, Dr. Jean Murphy, continued his ministry after his death. In a lecture she gave in 1986, quoting her late husband, she reiterated his philosophy:

I want to teach men and women of their Divine Origin, and the powers regnant within them. I want to inform that this power is within and that they are their own saviors and capable of achieving their own salvation. This is the message of the Bible and nine-tenths of our confusion today is due to wrongful, literal interpretation of the life-transforming truths offered in it.

I want to reach the majority, the man on the street, the woman overburdened with duty and suppression of her talents and abilities. I want to help others at every stage or level of consciousness to learn of the wonders within.

She said of her husband: "He was a practical mystic, possessed by the intellect of a scholar, the mind of a successful executive, the heart of the poet. His message summed up was: "You are the king, the ruler of your world for you are one with God."

❑❑❑